The Millionaire Witch

The Millionaire Witch

MARGARET STUART BARRY

ILLUSTRATED BY LINDA BIRCH

COLLINS

First published in Great Britain by
HarperCollins Publishers Ltd 1992

Text copyright © Margaret Stuart Barry 1992
Illustrations copyright © Linda Birch 1992

ISBN 0 00 185470-4

A CIP record for this book is available from
the British Library

This book is set in Palatino

Printed and bound in Great Britain by

Contents

For Susan Dickinson

The Witch in Trouble

"George!" screamed the witch. "Have you eaten my pension book?"

George, the witch's cat, raised a filthy black eyebrow and ignored her. He was used to his mistress accusing him of evil crimes, like stealing and eating the furniture, and snoozing on her best Sunday knickers. He slunk away to a safer corner.

"If I can't find my pension book, I won't get no money, and that means no cat food for *you*."

George un-slunk himself from the safer corner and started to shove things around with his paw. He found lots of things he'd been looking for himself, like a rubber fish, the ON/OFF knob from the TV, and a half eaten mouse which was now so mouldy, not to mention annoyed looking, that George pushed the cushion back over it again. But he could not find anything that looked like a pension book.

"Useless as usual!" spat the witch. "I'm in a fine mess now. Without any money, I'll starve. I'll have the rent man locking me up. I'll have Lady Fox-Custard sneerin' at me and mockin' at me, and calling me a penniless old trampess. Oh! she'd love that!"

Her face was now ten shades of dark purple instead of its normal pale green and Simon, just arriving, wanted to know what was the matter with her.

"Plenty!" groused the witch. "I've gone and lost me pension book." She gave George another dirty look and had a quick glance down his throat and round his teeth to see if there were any traces of words and numbers sticking there.

"Gosh!" said Simon. "You'll never find it in this mess." He glanced around the witch's sitting room at the piles of strange objects which were stacked in every corner; at the large grey settee which looked like a lumpy squashed elephant, half buried under a mountain of woollen stockings.

"I don't know what you mean," sulked the witch.

"Anyway," Simon said, hastily, "you can just go down to the post office and tell them, and they'll give you another one."

"I know that," lied the witch. "I was just going to do it. Come on then." The witch did not approve of long queues, so she pushed herself up to the front.

"Hey!" cried everyone.

"I want a new pension book," she began.

"Can I see your old one, madam?" said the girl behind the counter.

"If you could see my old one, I wouldn't be wanting a *new* one, would I! The witch was getting irritable. She didn't like post office people. They made out that all the money under the counter was *theirs* and they were just giving you some of it because you were old, or poor, or scruffy – though not really worthy.

"Oh aye," scoffed the snooty post office girl, "and where did you lose it, lady?"

"I was riding up the front face of Everest on me motor bike and a gust of wind blew it out of me pocket. How do poor old ladies *usually* lose their pension books?"

"She'll get mad," whispered Simon.

"She *is* mad!" snorted the witch. "She wants to see a book I haven't got. And then she wants to know where I've lost it, and she's too stupid to know that if I knew where I'd lost it – then I wouldn't have lost the pesky thing in the first place, WOULD I?"

The people in the queue were getting impatient. They wanted stamps, and parcels weighing, and TV licences. The fat old woman in the black dress at the front of the queue was making them all late.

The post office girl gave the witch a form to fill in.

"Age?" asked the form.

"None of yer bloomin' bizness," scribbled the witch in her very worst handwriting.

"You can't put that!" exclaimed Simon.

The witch crossed out the answer and wrote "dunno", which was true.

She had no idea how old she was. She was at least a hundred. Maybe two hundred. Perhaps she was only twenty-four. A wisp of tatty grey hair fell over her eyes. "Well, perhaps not quite as young as that," she thought.

At that moment, Lady Fox-Custard zoomed up to the front of the queue beside the witch's and haughtied, "I want one thousand pounds. It's my grocery shopping day." She gave the witch a nasty sideways smile, brimful of snootiness.

The witch hastily asked for a dog licence.

"You don't need a licence for a dog anymore," whispered Simon, "and anyway, you haven't *got* a dog."

"Didn't have you mean," hissed the witch.

When she arrived home, the witch waved her magic wand at George and changed him into a dog. The dog turned out to be a large, stiff haired mongrel and she called him Boney.

"Miaow," said Boney, peevishly.

The witch was greatly amused, but then she became very glum. What was she to do? It would be ages before she got a new pension book. She had no savings. Her magic wand could do almost anything, but it was rotten at making money. Meanwhile she had to pay the rent and buy food.

"I'm a poor old widder woman," she wailed.

"You could get a job," said Simon.

The witch went pale.

"When people need money," Simon continued, "they go out to work."

"Work!" The witch turned even paler. "I'm . . . . I'm too busy," she declared.

"But you don't do *anything!*" gasped Simon.

"Yes I do," spat the witch. She thought frantically. "I grow cabbages, and nasturtiums." She was going to say she cleaned the house, but as she was leaning on a particularly fluffy piece of furniture, she merely added, "and there's George . . . . I mean Boney to feed. That animal takes a terrible lot of looking after."

"I don't know then," shrugged Simon. And he went home for his tea. How the witch would have loved some tea, but there was nothing in the cupboard. Not even a spider's leg, which she could have fried or sautéd in butter. Already she felt she was getting thinner. The mirror told her she wasn't. But then the mirror was cracked.

"Oh misery," moaned the witch, going to bed before "Neighbours" came on.

Next morning she put on her best dress – a dress sprinkled with dead moths, but with very few soup stains on it, and stamped off to the supermarket.

"I want to see the manager," she demanded, snappishly.

"You mean, *please*," said the doorman. "Haven't you any manners?"

"If I lived in a manor, I wouldn't be coming to a dump like this," snorted the witch. "Only *posh* people have manors. Where's the manager?"

"Have you got a complaint?" sighed the doorman.

"Did have," answered the witch, "but I put ointment on it and it's much better now. Not that that's any business of yours."

"Oh dear!" thought the doorman. "Why do I get all the nutters? Must be because it's Friday the thirteenth." And he led the witch to an office where the manager was extremely busy drinking tea.

"A lady to see you, sir," he said, and hurried away.

The witch sat down and helped herself to a cup of tea.

"I want some money," she said.

The manager trembled. Was this one of those terrible hold-ups one read about so much?

He stared at the witch's dress and wondered about all the dead moths. She was obviously a vicious old woman; dangerous. A murderer perhaps. He looked nervously across his desk to see how far away the telephone was. If he grabbed it and dialled the police, would she draw a knife on him – or even a gun?

"A job," the witch went on.

Some pink blood came back into the manager's face. "Oh! A job!" he choked. "For a minute, I thought . . . "

"And I need it *now*. Just show me where the till is."

"No, no," said the manager. "You can't have a job. We don't need anyone."

The witch was running back into the shop.

"Yes, you do, she snapped. "Don't tell such fibs. *There's* an empty till."

And she leapt into the driving seat and started to hammer away at the buttons.

"Eeeeh!" screeched Doreen, who was on the next till, and busy dropping eggs into the money drawer in her fright.

"PLEASE! MADAM!" bellowed the manager. "Will you kindly leave that till alone."

"I'm just showing you I can do the job," said the witch. "It's easy peasy . . . Best steak, £60 a pound; cat food, tuppence a tin; cabbages' five pounds each; black stockings, one penny a pair . . . . AND I don't drop eggs everywhere like that one there!"

Doreen said "Eeeeh," again, and the false eyelashes she was wearing, batted like a pair of terrified spiders.

"She's all to pot!" thought the witch, scornfully.

A small boy arrived at the counter. He had a tin of coke which he had opened and half drunk.

"That tin's half empty!" exclaimed the witch. "You can have it for half price." The boy looked astonished and ran off to tell his friends.

"You're ruining me!" gasped the manager, aghast.

"I never even touched you," said the witch. "You was a ruin when I came in. I'm glad I did come though. You need helpin'. That one there's no good." She gave Doreen another scornful look.

Doreen began to sniffle and say that she wanted to give in her notice.

The witch grabbed a box of tissues from the shelf. "I was only kidding," she said. "Ere, have these on the house and cheer up."

Out of nowhere, a large queue of small boys
arrived at the witch's till. They were clutching half-
eaten bars of chocolate; open tins of fizzy drinks,
some of them already empty; apples with large
bites out of them; packets of almost finished crisps;
and a large assortment of damaged toys.

"Good Gordon!" gasped the witch. "What a
rotten shop this is – all of them things a mess.
I never seen the likes of it. You can 'ave 'em all
for nothing. I'm not charging for that lot!"

The boys shot off, delighted, and re-entered the
shop at the other end. A few adults shifted over
into the witch's queue, looking greedily hopeful.
Unnoticed by the witch, who by now was thor-
oughly enjoying her new job, the manager had slid
off and was returning with two very large men.
They were known in the town as Cosh and Carry.
Both of them looked nastily at the witch.

"All right then, Granny," they said. "Out you
go."

"Hey up!" cried the witch, as she was scooped
out of her chair. "Where are we going?"

"Walkies," said Cosh.

"Outy outy," said Carry.

"But I haven't had me wages yet!" screeched the
witch, struggling to kick Cosh and punch Carry.

"You're *sacked!*" boomed the manager, hiding
behind Doreen.

"Murder! Police!" yelled the witch, then, remem-
bering that she wasn't very friendly with some of
the police, added, "Mummy!"

Cosh and Carry dumped the witch on the pavement, where they left her in a most difficult position, showing large acres of navy blue knicker.

"Good heavens!" exclaimed Simon, appearing with his mother's shopping list, "what on earth are you doing there?"

"I'm sunbathing," growled the witch. "What does it look as if I'm doing?"

"But it's raining." said Simon.

"So it is," said the witch, rubbing her green nose on the back of her sleeve. "I must've dozed off."

And she went home, sulking.

'Sic Animuls'

Fortunately for George, the witch discovered a tin of cat food in her hat.

"It must've dropped in by mistake," she lied to herself. "That dozy Doreen must've knocked it in when she threw all them eggs around the shop."

To make up for this dreadful lie, the witch decided to share the cat meat with Boney. Now that he had doggy teeth instead of pussy teeth, he was unable to nibble the furniture as he usually did when he was hungry.

Boney wagged his tail and purred and felt confused. He wished he could be a cat again – a stupid feeling of friendliness kept stealing over him and he didn't feel normal.

"You're *not* normal," snapped the witch. "You're even uglier than you used to be, and you don't take yourself for walks like you used to."

"Wuff," miaowed Boney, almost pleasantly.

"How I wish I'd never showed off in the post office – pretending I needed a dog licence. If that stuck up Lady Fox-Custard hadn't come in, I wouldn't have needed to do that."

She wondered what her many witch relatives would think if they saw her flying through the air with a DOG stuck on the back of her broomstick. She could pretend it was a new fashion, of course. She could tell them they were all dead old-fashioned. It was only in stupid fairy stories that witches had to have cats on their broomsticks. Who had made up the rotten rule anyway? If she cared to, she could have a crocodile with purple teeth – none of her relatives could beat that!

Her dream was interrupted by a miaow outside her front door.

"A tiger, no doubt," thought the witch.

She whisked open the door, prepared for battle, but there was nothing to be seen except for a lump of gingery fur on the doorstep.

"That's funny!" cried the witch. "I never ordered no rug. I couldn't afford the pesky thing."

The "rug" twitched and then rolled over with a pitiful cry, so that the witch could see four legs sticking up in the air, like worn-out bottle brushes. At one end of it was a pink nose; the nose seemed to have a streaming cold. And at the other end, drooped a mangled tail.

"Crikey!" said the witch. "I'd swear that was a cat!"

She scooped it up and brought it indoors. Then

she switched on the star in her kitchen and saw that what she had found was indeed a cat.

Was it alive or was it dead? That was the question.

In the back of her fridge was a stale bottle of milk. There was very little left, but she poured it down the creature's throat, and at once, the animal opened its mouth and sat up.

"I've been conned!" fumed the witch. "Boney and I could've had that milk in our tea! This thievin' beast, pretending to be a dead moggy, thinks me house is a bloomin' hospital . . . HOSPITAL!" the witch hooted. "If this ignorant, moth eaten, ginger apology of a cat, this cunning, deceitful, little varmint thinks me house is a hospital – then maybe it *could* be. What an idea! A pet's hospital. A ten star hotel for sick animals!"

She sat down at once to make a sign. In no time at all, she had hammered it onto her front gate. It read,

Hospitul For Sic Animuls
Luckshree Beds
Medsun and Bandujes
ONLEE TEN Pounds a NITE
Expurt Attenshun.

When Simon arrived, the witch had hastily made a cot. She was busy wrapping up the cat (whose name was Ginger believe it or not) with a somewhat greyish looking blanket, and was tucking him up.

"What's this?" exclaimed Simon.

"Shush," warned the witch. "It's nearly lights out. This poor old, dear, little pussy cat is sick. It's got pneumonia."

Simon stared at the cat, which now had its whiskers sticking over the blanket, and was grinning, cosily.

"It's terrible sick," said the witch.

"Oh," said Simon, puzzled.

At that moment, Boney limped in. He had all four paws bandaged. His tail was in a splint, and he wore a patch over one eye.

"And what on earth's the matter with *him?*" gasped Simon.

"Nothin'!" hissed the witch, "but it looks good for business. I've just started a hospital for sick animals. These are my first two patients."

"You're bonkers," Simon wanted to say, but the witch's face was brilliant green, which meant she was in the middle of one of her brilliant ideas, so he said, "Who do you think is going to come here?"

"COME here!" boomed the witch. "How many sick animal hospitals do you know in this town?"

Simon couldn't think.

"How many animal doctors are there?"

Simon still couldn't think.

"You can't say, can you?" said the witch, gleefully. "That's because there *aren't* any. I'm the only animal doctor in this town. I'm the only one who's got a hospital for them. All those poorly sick, nearly dead creatures – there must be millions of them."

Simon was silent. His own tortoise was a bit peeky, and Jimmy's goldfish had a habit of dying, but he couldn't imagine that there were millions of sick animals in the town. The witch however, did need a job, so he said, "I suppose I could bring Dozey."

"Who's Dozey," asked the witch, who was deep in a book of witch medicine, entitled, *Ancient and Modern Cures for Man and Beast.*

"He's my tortoise," said Simon.

"Bring him along," said the witch, "but don't forget it's ten pounds a night."

"But I don't get ten pounds a *year!*" exclaimed Simon, indignantly.

As Simon was the witch's very best friend, she added, "Well, he can come as an out-patient then."

To the witch's astonishment, quite a few pets

started to arrive. Her tiny kitchen was soon quite full of growling, squeaking, snoring animals. Simon's tortoise had been shoved on to the mantelpiece. When Jimmy arrived with his sick goldfish, there was no room for the bowl so she emptied it into the sink.

"There's washing up liquid in there!" complained Jimmy.

"Well," said the witch, "I like my patients to be clean. The water you brought him in was so mucky, I couldn't tell whether he was a goldfish or a sardine."

"What's wrong with him then?" Jimmy sulked.

The witch thought frantically. "He's got fungus on his fin," she decided.

"It looks to me like a piece of potato peeling," said Jimmy, nervously.

"Well it *would* look like that to you," scoffed the witch. "That's because *you're* not a doctor like I am."

Meanwhile, Boney was getting squashed out of his own home. He had his front paws on the doormat, and his back paws in the yard.

"Trust him!" sighed the witch. "If he was a cat again, I could shut the door."

"I think," said Simon, "you should build some kennels outside."

"I'd just thought of that idea myself," lied the witch. "Your tortoise can go out for a start, seeing how he's only an out-patient anyway," she added, sniggering at her own joke.

As it was a Saturday morning, Simon and Jimmy were quite glad of something to do. There were kennels and cages to be made.

"A pond would be good in case we get any alligators", suggested the witch.

Simon said nothing. He knew when the witch was in one of her showing off moods. Jimmy borrowed some of his father's tools and was busy making them blunt.

"I'd better make some labels," said the witch, who wasn't keen on woodwork. "Then I'll know, without looking in, what different diseases each animal's got".

With her tongue poked out, so that she could write neatly, she wrote, CAT MEEZLES, DOG-AIK, RABBIT ROOMATISM, TAIL ROT, GON MAD.

The witch was not sure exactly what kind of medicine to give the animals, so she made pots of tea, mixed it with lemonade, and then magicked a nasty taste into it – just so that everyone would know that it was *real* medicine.

To her surprise, some of the animals started to get better. And even more surprising, their owners paid her the money and took them home. Even Simon was impressed.

"She's really quite a kind old lady," his mother said.

But the witch was finding it harder than she had expected to look after so many animals. Half of them, she didn't even like, especially the large, black mongrel called Growly, whose kennel had got GON MAD written over it. For Growly kept trying to leap over the yard wall and with each leap, he managed to reach higher.

"I'll miss the lemonade out of his medicine,"
the witch decided. "The fizz is making him too
bouncy."
   She also decided to put some barbed wire on top

of the wall. That should stop the wretched creature from escaping . . . She had just finished this job when a lady called Mrs Fuller-Tankerville arrived. She opened the boot of her car and lifted out a sick parrot.

"Now I would like to ask you a few little questions," she started.

"Ask away," said the witch, rattling her stethoscope.

"Are the animals cleaned every day?" said Mrs Fuller-Tankerville.

"Yes," said the witch. (She'd stick Jimmy's goldfish into a vase and swish the parrot in some fairy liquid.)

"And what kind of medicine would you be giving him?"

"Depends what he's got, Mrs – apart from feathers and a beak that is," the witch cackled.

Mrs Fuller-Tankerville frowned. If there had been another animal hospital in the town, she would have taken her parrot away, but there wasn't, so she didn't. "He's stopped talking," she explained. "He used to speak so beautifully. He used to say 'please' and 'thankyou' and 'may I leave the room?'."

"Oh," said the witch, who was glad the boring bird wasn't *her* pet. "We'll soon have him chatting away again. I'll learn 'im all right."

She did some quick money sums in her head then said, "It might take me a week, though."

"Oh, I'd pay *anything*," chirped Mrs Fuller-Tanker-ville, "just so long as my darling Polly will speak to me again."

"Might take *two* weeks, even," added the witch.

She squeezed the parrot into a cage along with a few other birds, and when it refused to say 'thankyou,' she shuffled off to see if Growly was still in his kennel. Luckily, the non-fizzy medicine seemed to have worked, for the dog was lying there, sulking.

Each evening after school, Simon and Jimmy went along to help the witch. They found it was quite exciting. Jimmy's goldfish was swimming round very fast.

"How did you get him to do that?" Jimmy asked.

"Easy," boasted the witch. "I gave him a rubber shark to play with and he just started rushing around like that. You must keep giving him toys."

On the other hand, Simon's tortoise had not moved.

"They have pot ones down at the garden centre," huffed the witch. "Are you sure *that's* not a pot one?"

"Pot tortoises don't eat lettuce!" exclaimed Simon, indignantly.

"Oh well then," the witch shrugged, "If you're absolutely *certain* it's real, then I'm afraid there's nothing I can do for him. S'no wonder you call him Dozey. And if he's going to carry on like that, – taking up a hospital bed, you might as well take him home."

"After all I've done to help her!" grumbled Simon, as he and Jimmy wandered home to finish their homework.

"Yes," said Jimmy, trying not to slop his goldfish out of its jar.

"And do you know," Simon went on, "she's making heaps of money. She's got it all in a stocking at the foot of her bed."

Simon was getting crosser, so Jimmy said, "I think your tortoise is just asleep. Tortoises do that sort of thing. Do you think my goldfish would like a plastic mermaid to play with?"

In spite of his bad mood, Simon went back to see the witch the next day. His mother had given him a scrap of meat for Growly. When he arrived, the witch was reading the dictionary to Polly, the parrot.

"This is the dumbest parrot I ever met!" she grumbled.

Suddenly, Boney limped across the room to the door. He sniffed. There was a smell under it which he seemed to recognize. But he couldn't decide whether he liked it or he didn't, so he gave a purry sort of wuff, meaning, it could be a friend or it could be an enemy.

"What's up now?" groaned the witch.

She waddled across the kitchen and flung open the door. On the step stood eight gorillas: Banana, Crumpet his wife, and six baby gorillas. Banana had a letter stuck behind one ear. He plucked it out and handed it to the witch.

Dear Sister of mine,
i red in the jungul express,
that yoo had started a hospitul
for sick animuls so here is a
few for yoo to practis on. Banana's
O.K. but his wife crumpet, and the
sicks children hav not been to wel laytlee
i expect the rest will do them gud.
Yor luving sister—Tombola
x x x x x x x x x x

"Oh NO!" exclaimed the witch.
The letter explained,

"REST!" shrieked the witch," it's ME who wants
the rest – sending me all her rotten gorillas so's that
she can just lie back in the sun, doing nuthin'."

Boney, however, was delighted to see Banana
again. Banana was full of joy. He was flinging his
arm around Crumpet and introducing his babies,
who were leaping around and going berserk and
saying hullo to all the sick animals, then hugging
and kissing them better.

"Lor' sakes!" exclaimed the witch.

Polly, who had been squashed flat in a cage full of
other birds, most of them common looking pigeons
with not a lot to say, started to polish his feathers.
There was something about Banana and Crumpet
and their rumbustious babies which struck a cord.

In his long distance memory, he could remember the squawks of his ancestors in the jungle; his multi-coloured gran and grandad – flying free and airily over the jungle trees.

"Squawk," he chirped. "Who's a pretty boy, then? Please. Thankyou. Shut the door."

"Gosh!" exclaimed Simon. "That medicine's working."

"Of course it is," said the witch, very surprised. When Mrs Fuller-Tankerville came to collect her silly bird, she would no doubt go round telling everybody what a fantastic animal doctor, she, the witch, was.

There was a knock at the door and the witch, stuffing the parrot under one arm, rushed to open it. But instead of Mrs Fuller-Tankerville, a strange little man stood on the doorstep. He was wearing a dark suit, a clean shirt, and a huge pair of spectacles through which he stared, strictly, at the witch.

"I am Bilge from the Planning Department," he told her.

"Where's yer sick animal?" the witch asked.

"I haven't got one," scowled Mr Bilge. "I've come about your yard."

"It's full of poorly creatures," the witch said.

"I *know*." Mr Bilge frowned again. "That's why I've come. You didn't get Planning Permission to turn your yard into a hospital."

"Didn't *need* it," grinned the witch. "Any idiot . . . I mean, anybody with brains like I've got could turn a yard into a hospital – for sick animals I mean."

"You should have asked permission," Mr Bilge went on.

"Who's he?" asked the witch.

"And I don't like all that barbed wire on the top of your wall. It's dangerous."

At that moment, Growly made the most enormous leap at the yard wall.

"You see what I mean!" gasped Mr Bilge. "What is that unfortunate animal trying to do?"

"Oh, you mean Growly," exclaimed the witch. "What a *lovely* dog he is. He's practising jumping for the Olympics. He's getting better every day."

She patted Growly affectionately on the end and booted him back into his kennel.

"What a dear beast he is!" she added.

"It looked to me as if he was trying to *escape!*" Mr Bilge went on, sternly.

"Oh dear me no!" flustered the witch.

"I'm sure he *was,*" snapped Mr Bilge, "and I wouldn't blame him. You've no right to keep so many animals in such a small back yard."

The witch was beginning to feel very cross, and also a bit worried. She spread out her skirt in front of the pigeon cage, hoping that Mr Bilge would not see that there were at least fifty of them and six baby gorillas playing Pull-The-Dicky-Birds-Tails.

"No room. No room!" squawked Polly.

"Who said that?" rounded Mr Bilge.

"Squashy! Squashy!" Polly shrieked.

"It came from behind your skirt," Mr Bilge snapped.

He pushed the witch to one side and opened the cage. Out shot the fifty pigeons, followed by Polly, and then the six baby gorillas, laughing fit to choke themselves.

"My goodness!" exploded Mr Bilge. "Did all that lot come out of one cage?"

"Well, there is a sort of long tunnel behind it with passageways leading off into a large . . ."

"RUBBISH!" roared Mr Bilge. "I'm going to have this dreadful place closed down at once. And what's more, you will get a large fine."

"I'll get a fine what?" stammered the witch.

"A FINE!" bellowed Mr Bilge. "That means you will have to pay me a lot of money for breaking the law."

"The only thing I ever broke in my life was a cup," moaned the witch.

"Arrrrrrrh!" roared Mr Bilge, stamping out.

Banana came and put his arm round the witch and Crumpet made a pot of tea. The baby gorillas played a quiet game of Ludo, and behaved considerately.

"I had a feeling it wasn't a very good idea," Simon mumbled.

"It was a *super* idea," snapped the witch. "I'm just a poor old lady, tryin' to make a livin' until that nosey parker came along."

The very next morning, Mr Bilge's fine plopped through the letter box.

Banana smelt it and pulled a face.

"Two hundred pounds!" the witch gasped.

"You'll have to pay it, I'm afraid," said Simon, "or you'll go to prison. And you'll have to get rid of all the animals too."

The witch was now sick of her hospital anyway. The animals were more trouble than they were worth. They were fed up with the tea and lemonade medicine and were beginning to spit it out, or to use it for washing their whiskers. Growly had become so wild, that not even Banana could hold him down. The witch wrote a note and hastily pinned it on her front gate. It said,

This hospitul is clozin
plees cum anb colekt yor
petts.
All of them is betta
i hav querd them
sined Maytrun.
P.S. Sum of yoo still owe too hundRid pounds.

A queue of cars rolled up to the witch's gate, and one by one the animals were taken away. Growly leapt into the driving seat next to his mistress and barked joyfully all the way home.

Mrs Fuller-Tankerville was the last to arrive.

The witch grabbed the parrot by the neck and carried it out to the car.

"How do you do," greeted the parrot.

"Oh! Polly my darling!" twittered Mrs Fuller-Tankerville. "You can *talk* again!"

Polly spat a few green feathers at the car, followed by a pink and blue one.

"Flippin' hec!" he swore. "Knickers, knickers."

"Oh my goodness!" gasped Mrs Fuller-Tankerville. "What have you done to my sweet little bird?"

"Learnt him to talk again," grumped the witch.

"You're a wicked woman!" screamed Mrs Fuller-Tankerville as she drove off.

"Witch! Witch!" called Polly, spitting one last orange feather out of the car window.

"Golly!" exclaimed the witch. "How ungrateful some people are."

"You'd better come back into the kitchen, quickly," shouted Simon. "The baby gorillas are up to something."

The baby gorillas were in a heap on top of Boney, gibbering excitedly and tweaking his tail.

When the witch managed to pull them off, she found to her amazement that Boney, the dog, had turned back into George, the cat.

"Oh joy!" cried the witch, hugging him to her bosom. "It must've been my tea and lemonade medicine. What a wonderful doctor I am!"

George slunk under the settee. He'd had a nightmare, he was sure. His house had been full of mad dogs, and parrots, and pigeons, and mouldy goldfish, and sick tortoises, and he fancied, in his nightmare, that he had been a horrid dog.

"Oh joy!" exclaimed the witch again.

The Witch at Sea

The witch, who didn't fancy going to prison, especially when she heard that cats were not allowed, paid her fine to Mr Bilge.

"And now I'm poor again," she groaned to Simon.

"Hasn't your new pension book arrived?" he asked.

"No," sighed the witch. "And neither has Christmas!"

"Perhaps you should go to the Job Centre," suggested Simon.

"Been," snapped the witch. "They say I'm too old."

Simon stared at the witch; her long black dress, which was never without soup stains, trailed across the floor. Her face, which had a greenish look, was half hidden by a mass of tangled grey hair, which lay across her shoulders like a flock of sick seagulls.

And her shoes looked like huge boats that were about to set sail across the Atlantic.

"Perhaps," he hesitated, "if you were to smarten yourself up a little . . ."

"Smarten?" growled the witch.

"Well, dress a little younger," Simon finished.

"I'm not *that* old," sniffed the witch.

She still couldn't call to mind whether she was a hundred, or two hundred, or even three hundred. Her mother, who had been called Bunty the Broom, had died when the witch was only two and left behind no birth certificate. There had been a letter from Napoleon the Great, but Bunty the Broom had carelessly slopped gravy over it, so even this clue had been lost.

"My mother said I mustn't be late for tea," said Simon hastily, escaping quickly.

"Too old," muttered the witch. "Not smart enough."

Her eye fell upon a woman's magazine, in which she had wrapped up the potato peelings. There were some silly pictures of silly young girls in it. As far as the witch could see, the girls looked like clowns. They had frocks above their knees; eyelashes like overgrown spiders' legs; and their hair, which was of various unlikely colours, looked as if it had just been electrocuted.

"Oh well," thought the witch, "If that's what being young looks like . . . Gloria," she read on, "has just been made an MP. Mad Pumpkin, I suppose," guessed the witch.

Member of Parliament, the magazine went on.

"Golly!" cried the witch. "This lark looks easy. I could do as good as them."

She pulled up the bath tub in front of the fire, emptied the remains of the lemonade medicine into it, and sat in it until she was nearly white. In order not to waste the water, she threw in her black dress and underclothes. Meanwhile, she took down her wand and opened up her Magic Spell Book. She looked up the letter Y for Young, and D for Dress, and suddenly she was standing in a yellow dress of swishy silk. The witch regarded herself in the mirror.

"Crumbs!" she chortled.

The dress was very short, and the witch could not remember the last time she had seen her knees. They were horribly bony and bumpy, but by the time she had glued a few sequins to them, they looked quite nice. Lastly, she dyed her hair a cheerful pink. All that was left to be done was to powder her nose and paint her mouth orange.

George crawled out from under the settee, meaning to hint for some dinner, but at the sight of the witch, he shot back underneath again.

"He's dazzled by me beauty," giggled the witch, setting off at once to the Job Centre.

Immediately, the witch espied the job she fancied. It was printed on a neat card at the front of the window and read,

WANTED. A LIVELY YOUNG GIRL TO WORK
AS A HOSTESS ON A WORLD CRUISE. MUST
BE PRETTY AND UNDER TWENTY-ONE.

The witch, who was wearing very high heels,
staggered through the doorway. "I've come about
the job," she said.

"*Which* job?" asked the girl behind the counter,
startled by the witch's appearance.

"No, not a *witch* job, the world cruise job."

"Er . . ." said the girl. She had never seen hair
as pink as the witch's. She wondered if her own
would go that colour, but maybe her boyfriend
would drop her if it did.

"It hasn't gone, has it?" snapped the witch.

"No, not yet, but . . ." The girl was dazzled by
the swishiness of the witch's yellow silk dress
and by the sequins on her knees. Perhaps, she
thought, she had come straight from Top Of The
Pops studio.

"Are you under twenty-one?" she asked.

"Am I under twenty-one *what*" demanded the
witch. This Job Centre girl was getting on her
nerves. She didn't seem to know what she was
talking about – asking if she was under twenty-
one without saying whether she meant elephants,
banana trees or sticky buns. The witch decided to
be patient.

"You've got a job. And it's for a hostess on a
world cruise. And it's for a beautiful young girl.
And nobody's taken it?"

The girl nodded and shook her head.

"Right," said the witch. "Then I'll take it."

The girl nodded again, and gave the witch a card, telling her that she started next week.

Joyfully, the witch raced round to see Simon.

Simon was doing his homework and looked startled.

"It's *me!*" whooped the witch.

"Golly!" exclaimed Simon.

"I look lovely, don't I?" the witch went on, excitedly. "And next week, I'm going on a world cruise, so I won't see you for a bit."

"What about Banana, and Crumpet and the babies?" asked Simon, still shocked.

"I'll take them with me," said the witch, who had forgotten all about Tombola's pets in her excitement. "The ship is bound to go near Africa, so I can drop them off."

The day of sailing arrived at last and the witch had packed her magic wand, made a few more twinkly dresses and left a pile of sawdust in the fridge for George. The baby gorillas had been put into clean nappies, and Banana and Crumpet carried the suitcases. They arrived at the harbour five minutes early.

The captain was on board, pacing up and down on deck and grinning at the passengers who were all rich.

"I'm your new hostess," puffed the witch, staggering up the gang plank. "I'm takin' charge of

fun and games, and swimming and diving, and parties."

The captain, who never in his life had been lost for words, was lost for them now.

The witch unpacked the gorillas and explained they would be getting off at Africa.

The ship started to move, so there was no time for the captain to radio the Job Centre and say that there had been a terrible mistake. Instead, he was obliged to hand the witch a list of passengers on board ship. "We have some very important people on this cruise," he groaned. "We have the Count and Countess of Numbahs, Field Marshall and Mrs Mud-Wellington, the Prince and Princess Pooftah, and Lady Fox-Custard."

"Lady Fox-Custard, did you say!" gasped the witch. Her white face powder fell off and turned green.

"Yes indeed, and she's a most charming lady," added the captain, "and I would not like to see her upset."

The witch was aghast. Lady Fox-Custard was her worst favourite person. To think that she had set sail on the seven seas, only to come up against her worst enemy.

"She even went to see the Queen," bragged the captain.

"I know she did," the witch said. "She seen her through the railings."

Just then, Lady Fox-Custard herself came wobbling down the deck. She was swinging a tennis racket and wearing a white mini skirt. Her fat legs shook like jellies.

"Hi there!" she greeted, playfully. "You must be the new hostess. I hope we're going to have lots of jolly fun."

"Oceans of it," grinned the witch, enormously pleased that Fox-Custard had not recognised her. "I thought we'd start off tonight with a fancy dress party."

"Super! And will the prize be to sit at the captain's table for dinner?"

"That's 'xactly what I had in mind," lied the witch.

Lady Fox-Custard's face lit up like a giant pumpkin and she hurried away to her cabin to make plans. She was already deeply in love with the captain and intended to win.

She emptied her suitcase onto the bed and sighed with delight at the sight of all the lovely dresses she possessed, not to mention her diamonds – well at least they *looked* like diamonds, anyway. What could she dress up as? She tottered along to the ship's library to look at picture books. There was Little Red Riding Hood . . . but then some nasty rough man might come as the wolf. That would never do. Perhaps she could go as a battleship. The mayor had once told her she looked like a battleship; but then she would not be able to wear her diamonds. "I've got it!" she shrieked, startling a little man who was showing off by reading a book. "I'll go as a fairy queen."

Meanwhile, the witch was squeezing into a sailor suit.

"Fancy getting *paid* for doing such an easy job," she tittered.

She rang her cabin bell to order a strawberry trifle.

"*Another* one?" gasped the waiter, who had been running from the galley to the witch's cabin all day.

"Is there a law against it?" huffed the witch. "Who's countin' anyway?"

"I am," muttered the waiter, as he beetled off to fetch the witch her ninetyeth trifle. "She was a bloomin' funny, not ha ha hostess!" he thought.

The moon popped up over the fo'c's'le and

the dancing began. The Count and Countess of Numbahs had come as a doctor and nurse. The Mud-Wellingtons as a couple of horses. The Prince and Princess of Pooftah had arrived as a palace on wheels, although the princess of course, was still wearing her diamonds under the battlements. As well as these, there were Red Indians, girls in grass skirts, white rabbits with watches, and a great many swashbuckling pirates.

"My goodness!" wheezed Lady Fox-Custard, "just wait till they see ME!"

She had put on twenty sticky-out petticoats, over which she had squashed a dress of gold satin. On her back, were safety-pinned a pair of wings she had made from cling film, and glued to her head

was a crown of diamonds. She waited for a new tune to start, then she teetered down the staircase.

Everybody gasped.

"How common!" whispered the palace on wheels.

"What a tart!" hooted the witch to herself.

"Sink me lifeboats!" thought the captain. "Collapse me telescope!"

"Lady Fox-Custard was delighted. She *felt* like a fairy queen. She could see that everyone was taken aback and was sure that she would win the prize.

While all this was going on, the baby gorillas were sitting at the bar, drinking coke and enjoying themselves as they had never done before. There were also two grown up gorillas, Fox-Custard noticed. Their costumes did not look awfully real, she thought; old and dusty. Probably from one of the cheaper hire outfitters. The biggest gorilla was asking her to dance. His breath smelt of jungle garbage. But Banana grabbed Fox-Custard round the waist, breathing heavily and squashing her wings.

"Oh my!" gasped Lady Fox-Custard, who *loved* strong men.

Banana grinned, and his teeth shone like yellow piano keys. He whizzed Lady Fox-Custard around the dance floor and hurled her recklessly into a rubber plant. One cling film wing fell off, but Lady Fox-Custard was too excited to notice.

"And now," said the witch, who had just had a brilliant idea, "we will make our way to the swimming pool."

"Oh what fun!" thought the baby gorillas, who badly needed a bath.

"*Surely* we must be getting near to Africa?" moaned the captain to the first mate.

"Line up!" screeched the witch. "You are all going to walk the plank."

She bounced up and down on the diving board like a navy-blue yo-yo.

"I want all the 'pirates' at the bouncy end to wobble the plank. Anyone who manages not to fall in has won the prize and will sit at the captain's table for dinner tonight."

The girls in grass skirts fell into the swimming pool almost immediately.

"Drat!" thought the captain.

The Mud-Wellingtons in their horse costumes fared no better.

"We're jolly old *sea* horses!" neighed Mrs Mud-Wellington, striking out to the side.

The palace on wheels was so heavy it sank without trace.

Soon, there was nobody left except the fairy queen.

"Oh my!" trembled Lady Fox-Custard, blushing and glancing at the captain.

"Just a minute," yelled the witch. "This competition is too easy. Blindfold that woman."

The pirates knotted a red spotted handkerchief over Lady Fox-Custard's eyes. Using her magic wand, the witch gleefully swung the diving board from the swimming pool over the stormy sea.

"I'm ready," warbled Lady Fox-Custard, picking her way carefully along the plank.

She swayed on her high heels. The waves boiled below her. And a flock of excited seagulls swooped around her diamond tiara.

"Bounce!" the witch ordered the pirates.

"Ooops!" yelled Lady Fox-Custard, flying up in the air above the seagulls and then disappearing beneath the waves.

"That's torn it," gasped the captain. "Man, I mean Lady overboard!"

Lady Fox-Custard had paid a lot of money to come on the cruise. She might never come again. Worse, she might tell the Queen – that is if the sharks didn't get her first. "Save that woman," he yelled.

Unfortunately, the witch had forgotten that the lady was her worst enemy. She could not help showing off and dived into the raging sea and grabbed Lady Fox-Custard by the hair. Bravely, she stabbed a hopeful shark with her wand and killed it. She could hear cheering from the deck, but she did not notice that the water was doing something awful to her disguise. The pink dye in her hair was fading, her lipstick turned green, and her false eyelashes floated away on the tide. Deprived of their plumptious lunch, the remaining sharks had to make do with eating the witch's sailor suit. She arrived back on board wearing nothing but her underwear and a mass of grey seaweedy hair.

"The WITCH!" screeched Lady Fox-Custard.

"Splice the mainbrace!" gasped the captain, not believing his eyes.

"Sack her!" hystericked Fox-Custard.

"You're sacked," spluttered the captain.

"What about me wages?" roared the witch.

"You're not getting any wages. I've a good mind to throw you overboard right now," bellowed the captain.

But the ship was not able to sail back to port, for a terrible storm blew up and not even the seagulls could stay in the air.

The captain locked the witch in her cabin and told her to behave.

"How can I behave?" grumbled the witch as the storm hurled her from one side of the cabin to the other. "How does he expect me to sit still and behave when the walls are leaping up and playing badminton with me?"

She wondered if everyone else on the ship was getting thrown about. So, using her magic wand as a key, she let herself out into the corridor. The corridor was just as bad and she crawled up the stairs on her hands and knees to the deck above. The deck was awash with people all rolling around and grabbing onto the railings.

"Aha!" chuckled the witch. "A jolly old thunder storm. What fun!"

Lady Fox-Custard rolypolyed past her, screeching in terror.

"Not a pretty sight!" chortled the witch, not trying to catch her.

"Where's the captain?" demanded Field Marshall Mud-Wellington.

"I'll go and see," said the witch, importantly. "I'm still the hostess so I'll go and find him."

The captain was on the bridge, hanging on to the helm and trying to turn it. "I feel sick," he groaned.

"You should eat something then," advised the witch. "I saw some cold custard left over in the kitchen."

"*Cold custard!*" shuddered the captain, turning yellow.

"Goodness!" said the witch. "You really do look sick. I'll drive the ship home for you."

"You don't know how. You stupid woman," the captain managed to grunt. "Haven't you noticed we're in the middle of a terrible storm?"

"S'nothin'," said the witch. "I'll soon learn how to drive this old boat. The storm's nothin'."

Suddenly, the captain had to leave and the witch took the helm. She whizzed it this way and that, and the boat lurched left and then right and nearly turned upside down.

"Golly!" said the witch. "It looked easy!"

She remembered learning when she was young that there were three important witches who were in charge of the weather. They were called Rosey Rumble, Betty Blow-Hard, and Pansy Puff. She left the helm to whizz round on its own and peered up at the sky.

"It's ME!" she shouted. "The witch. Will you give over rocking me boat?"

The weather witches looked down in surprise, rumbled to one another, and then blew off in the direction of the Bay of Biscay where they knew that sailors were more used to them.

The witch sailed the ship into port and the captain said, "Thank goodness for that – but don't think I'm not going to report you to the police."

"I should think so indeed!" snapped Lady Fox-Custard, who had lost her tiara overboard and was wearing a large lobster in her hair. "The police should give her the worst possible punishment. She should die a slow and 'orrible death."

"Oh, that's a bit rough, dear," gasped Mrs Mud-Wellington. "She's only a poor old lady really."

It was then that one of the passengers noticed that there were palm trees on the shore.

"Splice the flippin' mainbrace!" exclaimed the

captain in despair. "She's sailed us into a foreign port!"

"Yoo hoo!" shouted the witch, who had just spotted her sister Tombola driving a pick-up truck out of the jungle in order to collect her gorillas. Banana, Crumpet, and the six baby gorillas leapt into the waves and swam towards the shore where they hugged and kissed their dear mistress.

"Aaah," sighed Mrs Mud-Wellington. "Isn't that sweet!"

The journey home was a long one, and the witch carried on her duties as a hostess. She organised Snakes and Ladders competitions, crab races, and "Hunt the Shark".

Neither the captain nor Lady Fox-Custard joined in these jollifications, and when the ship arrived home, the witch hid in a crate of bananas and was safely delivered ashore.

As she was passed through customs, she could not resist poking her nose through the crate and hooting, "Have a banana!"

But the customs man decided that there was no such thing as a talking banana, so let her through.

A Job with
the Law

"I read about it in the papers," Simon told the witch when she arrived home from Africa. "Lady Fox-Custard has got 'flu. She is talking about having you sent to prison."

The witch sneezed and blew her nose on Simon's mother's tablecloth. "It's all right for her," she grumbled. "SHE doesn't have to worry about lost pension books. SHE doesn't have to bother about being a poor old woman with a starvin' cat."

"She's still getting the police round to your house, though," Simon went on.

"I'm sure they wouldn't send an old lady to prison," said Simon's mother, kindly.

But Simon was not so sure. His friend was not just any old lady, she was a witch, and she did things which ordinary old ladies would never dream of doing.

George, who had been left alone for a whole

week and finished the sawdust which the witch had left for him in the fridge, had eaten his way through most of her kitchen table. He had also eaten half of the front door, so that it was not too difficult for the police to walk in.

"I did not hear you knock," snapped the witch.

"There was nothing to knock at," sneered Inspector Finga Printz. "I have come to arrest you."

"What for?" the witch asked. She was peeling a large onion and the tears were beginning to roll down her face.

"You tried to drown Lady Fox-Custard," said the police inspector.

"No I never," cried the witch, crying a bit more.

"I saved her life. A shark was nearly going to eat her."

"Was it?" said Inspector Printz, wistfully. He didn't like Lady Fox-Custard himself. She was always ringing up the station, complaining: nasty boys had stolen her apples; there were burglars peering down her chimney pot, she had said; a dirty old tramp had had a bath in her goldfish pond – and so on. No, he didn't like Lady Fox-Custard at all. His bony body shuddered.

"Have you eaten today?" the witch asked him.

"I had a biscuit with my morning coffee," the inspector said.

"Tut, tut. I wonder you have the strength to arrest a flea! I was just about to cook some scrambled leg on toast. Would you like some?"

"I would that!" said Inspector Printz, sitting down at the remains of the table. He had had a terribly boring morning. He didn't fancy the scrambled leg, but he ate the toast hungrily. Then he had ten cups of tea, and wiped his moustache. "I don't suppose you *really* meant to push her Ladyship into the sea," he said.

"Of *course* I didn't," lied the witch. "I didn't really mean to save her either," she cackled.

She started to wash up, or rather, she put the plates on the floor for George to lick.

"That's a beautiful cat," remarked the inspector.

The witch stared at George. His hair was so tufty, he looked as if he'd had a bath in glue and forgotten to rinse it out. Five of his whiskers were bent, and his ears were alive with fleas. He was not a bit beautiful. She must have left dregs of the lemonade medicine in the inspector's cup and it had sent him ga-ga.

She polished the TV screen with some left-over stardust and arranged a bunch of rhubarb in a vase.

"How are you going to arrest me?" she asked casually.

"Oh!" the inspector shook himself. "I'm going to put these on you," he said. He produced a pair of handcuffs and snapped them onto the witch's wrists. At that moment Simon arrived. He was with his school friend, Jimmy.

"Oh golly!" cried Jimmy, trembling with fear.

"What's going on?" asked Simon.

"The inspector has just arrested me," grinned the witch.

Jimmy's face crumpled up. He liked the witch. He did not want to see her taken to prison. She was good fun.

"She's a very old woman," he stuttered.

"I'm not *that* much older than you!" objected the witch. "You should've seen me aboard that ship. I looked like a beautiful young girl. The captain nearly fell in love with me. And I'm jolly clever as well."

"Yes," agreed Jimmy. "She's awfully clever. She can do *anything*."

"Except get out of those handcuffs," laughed Inspector Printz. The witch's wand was still in her handbag which she had slung under the table. With one foot, she wriggled out of her boots and with her bare toes she managed to pick out her wand. She mutttered, secretly,

> "Fox-Custard is a snoopysnitch,
> But not as smart as me, the witch
> I am clever, I am bright,
> Vanish me handcuffs out of sight."

To everyone's amazement, the handcuffs began to melt. They made a fizzy noise, dribbled onto the floor, and were promptly licked up by George.

"Marvellous!" exclaimed Inspector Printz. "How did you do that?"

"Dunno," said the witch, who didn't.

"Of all the criminals I have arrested, no one has

been able to do that! You should be in the Police Force."

"Then she could catch the thief who stole my mummy's washing!" cried Jimmy. "They stole my school football shirt."

"Did they?" put in Simon. "My shorts have disappeared too!"

"This is serious!" exclaimed Inspector Printz, forgetting that the witch had tried to murder Lady Fox-Custard.

"Well as a matter of fact," said the witch, telling another of her enormous lies, "I have just applied for a job in the Police Force."

"I never seen your letter," said Inspector Printz. "Our postman is a bit potty," explained the witch. "I've seen him throwing letters in the ditch."

Inspector Printz had not had an important case for some time. He was sick of sitting in his office, filling in silly forms. He was sick of dashing out to Horty Hall and dragging naughty boys out of apple trees, and pulling harmless old tramps out of the goldfish pond, and getting haughtied at into the bargain. To catch a gang of washing-line thieves would be a big scoop. He might even get promoted to CHIEF Inspector.

"I never seen your letter," he said again, "but I'll let you join the Police."

"With a uniform?" asked the witch.

"Of course," said the inspector.

It took quite a long time to find a uniform large

enough to fit the witch, but at last one was found. It had extra buttons and extra badges. Also, she found a whistle in every pocket. To her great disappointment, she was not allowed to carry a machine gun, just a small pen and notebook.

"I feel stupid with a silly little notebook," sulked the witch.

"Never mind," said Simon. "You look terrific."

"Shouldn't we be getting a move on?" Jimmy said.

"WE!" scoffed the witch.

"I just thought . . ." Jimmy stuttered, "that seeing as how we're on half-term, maybe we could help you."

"And what do you suggest, bird brain?" poohed the witch.

"I thought we could hide in a few gardens and keep an eye on washing . . . on washing lines."

"You've been peeping in my notebook," huffed the witch. "That's just what I've gone and wrote down."

They spent an hour, squashed under one hedge, but nothing happened.

"Let's go down to New Road," suggested Simon.

The witch agreed. They settled down under another hedge and waited. Bored, the witch started to dig up worms. She was hungry.

Just then, Sally came out of her house. She was carrying a huge bag of washing.

"Hey up!" hissed the witch.

Sally, who did not like the witch one bit, snapped,

"What are you doing skulking about in our garden?"

"What are *you* doing, more like it?" the witch asked.

"I'm just off to the launderette, not that it's any business of yours. Nosey old hag."

"Aren't you going to hang it up here?" the witch wanted to know.

"What! In our garden. That would look common!" And off she went.

"Stuck-up little snoot!" muttered the witch. She began to think prison would be more exciting. "I thought being a policewoman would be more exciting than this," she grumbled.

"Police *person*, you mean," interrupted Jimmy.

The witch discovered that she had squashed a rose bush flat and thought it was time they moved on. Sally's mother would no doubt go on about it.

She was nearly as hoity toity as Lady Fox-Custard.

"We're not getting very far, are we?" complained Simon.

"I agree," said the witch, promptly leading them off to the Police Station.

Constable Fanny Foxtrot was on the desk, polishing her nails.

"Aw, hullo," she said.

"I want a police car," demanded the witch.

"What do you want it for?" asked Fanny Foxtrot, looking in alarm at the thumb nail which has just snapped.

"For chasing criminals in, of course," the witch spat.

"Aw," said Fanny. "Have you got a driving licence?"

"Well, of course I have!" said the witch. She did not tell the girl that her licence was only for driving her broomstick.

"You'll find one round the back in garage two."

"Eeeh!" cried Jimmy, as the witch started the car. "Are you sure you know how to drive this thing?"

"Certainly," answered the witch, switching on the windscreen wipers, the horn, and the lights, before she figured out how to get it going. One of the garge doors was still stuck to the bonnet as she zoomed off, but this soon fell off. Nair nair, nair nair, went the siren.

"Isn't this fun!" whooped the witch.

Simon and Jimmy were not so sure. In a way it

was, and in another way it wasn't. Shoppers were leaping out of the way. Lady Fox-Custard, who was on her way to the library, drove her Rolls-Royce into somebody's garden, taking a short cut through the hedge.

"Where are we going!?" puffed Jimmy.

"Dunno yet," said the witch. "Which of these three pedals do you think is the brake?"

"It's the MIDDLE one!" yelled Simon.

"So it is," giggled the witch, hurtling all three of them at the windscreen. "I think I've got the hang of it now. Driving a police car is easy peasy."

"We're supposed to be looking for washing line thieves," reminded Jimmy, clinging on and wishing he'd stayed at home – doing his holiday homework, even.

"So we are, midget brain," chortled the witch.

They were now speeding around the outskirts of the town, where some dismal little houses gave way to open fields, when a huge-policewoman-clue zoomed up ahead. It was a sportsground and a gang of small boys was playing football.

"Hullo, hullo, hullo!" hooted the witch, her eyes gleaming and her brain ticking fast.

Meanwhile, Inspector Printz, who had been told that there was a runaway police car causing trouble around the town, screeched to a halt behind the goal post at the same time as the witch.

"What have we here?" he boomed.

"If I'm not mistaken," said the witch, switching off her windscreen wipers, headlights, fog lights, and hazard lights all at the same time, "I think we have a clue to this case."

Inspector Printz could not see why, but he badly wanted to become Chief Inspector, so he said, "I do believe we 'ave," and rattled his handcuffs expertly.

He did not understand the witch and peered around, gormlessly.

"The clues are all out there," explained the witch, patiently, "and they're dashing around like a lot of monkeys, kicking some stupid ball."

"They're playing football," Simon told her. "It's the Blue Boys against the Basher Kids. It should be a good game!"

"Some game!" snorted the witch. "They've only got one ball."

"That's the whole idea," sighed Simon. "They've got to get it off one another and kick it into the net."

"Foul!" blew the referee.

"Ooh! they play with whistles too!" gleed the witch, blowing six of hers all at once.

Both teams started to run in all directions, shouting, "What's that? Where are we going? Stop pushing! Sir, they're cheating."

"You shouldn't have done that," groaned Jimmy.

"*He* did," sulked the witch, pointing a finger at the referee.

The game started again, and the Basher Kids were in good heart. The whistling and the fighting had got them all excited and ready to go.

"Goal!" yelled Billy Mac, leaping on top of all the other boys and kissing them.

"He's wearing my pants!" exclaimed Simon, flabbergasted.

"And that's my shirt!" squeaked Jimmy.

"Who? Which one? Where's he gone?" yelled the witch.

"He's right down there now, at the other end."

"Seen him!" bellowed the witch. And she leapt back into her car, switched the siren on, and sped across the pitch, doing expert wheelies to avoid killing any boys, and churning up the grass into deep ridges, as she went.

"Gotcha!" she yipped, snatching hold of the terrified Billy. "You're wearing stolen property!" she accused.

"Borrowed," whimpered Billy.

"Don't say anything now," warned the witch. "Those trousers is evidence."

"Are they?" stammered Billy Mac, confused. "I thought they was Marks and Spencers."

"Madam!" roared Inspector Printz, nearly shocked beyond words. "I must ask you to escort me back to the station."

"Why, what's the matter with your own car?" asked the witch, puzzled.

"It's in one piece for a start," snarled the inspector.

"What about the criminal I've just caught for you?" complained the witch, who still had hold of a wretched Billy Mac.

"Put him down. I'll deal with him later. It's *you* I want at the moment."

He bundled her into the car and drove off.

"Gosh!" What do you think will happen to her?" asked Simon.

"I expect she'll go to prison," answered Jimmy, astonished at the dreadfulness of it all.

It was, however, only a day later when they met the witch again.

"I'm out of the Police Force now," she said, unnecessarily. "They tried to fine me. But I couldn't pay it because I ain't got no money. And they wouldn't give me my wages, would you believe it. So they said they'd put me on probation this time, and I told them I'd willingly get on it if they just showed me what a probation *looked* like – and suddenly, they just told me to go home."

She gave them a handful of whistles each and went off, grinning.

The next day, Simon and Jimmy had their football clothes returned from Billy's mother. They were washed and ironed and came with a note, saying, that they had after all, only been *borrowed*, but that Billy had been forbidden to watch TV for the rest of the day and would never play football again. *Didn't want to play football ever again.*

The Witch and
the Tramp

The witch felt that she needed a rest from the hard job of being out of work. She had been insulted; fined; nearly sent to prison; and altogether discouraged. Even George seemed to have a better life than she did. He had just been to an auction sale at Sotheby's, and dined on some priceless Georgian furniture. Being very fleet of foot, he had escaped the auctioneer's hammer – which had been aimed viciously at his tail – and come home by rail on the roof of a first class compartment. He was now snoring contentedly in front of the fire, poofs of Georgian furniture blowing through his nose.

"Cats are not stupid!" grumbled the witch. "They don't have to go looking for work. They don't have to go trailing down to the job centre, like what I have to do. They don't have to use their brains, or think, or plot, or plan – they just *manage*."

There was nothing in the cupboard, so the witch

stumped into the garden in search of something to cook.

"I shall keep my poor body and soul alive with a boiled cabbage," she muttered.

But unfortunately, the slugs had got there first. They were full to bursting and trailing away towards the next door garden.

"Cheek of 'em!" complained the witch. "I shall just have to make do with a slug stew."

And she started to collect them.

She had scooped up no more than six, when she came across a large mound close to the nasturtium flowers. The large mound looked like a mackintosh. There was a hat at one end of it, and some large, dirty boots at the other. What's more, it was moving up and down as if it had breath in it. The witch poked it gently with a stick and a terrible roar came out of it. The mound as it happened was a tramp: dirty, red-faced, and heavily whiskered. His name was William.

"What the hec do you think you're doing - disturbing a man in the business of having a sleep?" yelled William.

"You're in my garden," spluttered the witch.

The tramp gazed about him "I thought it was a dump," he said. "I thought it was a slug zoo."

The witch was stuck for words. No one had ever dared to argue with her before. She stared hard at the tramp, who was still lying down, squashing her nasturtiums and not caring a bit. Here was a man she could admire. She admired the dirt on his face; the tattiness of his whiskers; the filth on his mackintosh and the blackness of his toenails, which were sticking through his boots. Most of all, she admired the way he said he would be glad to join her in a meal of slug stew.

"William," she said, when they had licked their plates clean and she had told him all about how poor she was, "how do *you* manage to make a living?"

"I don't *make* a living, I just waits and sees, and brilliant ideas hit me on the head."

The witch was interested but was still looking puzzled.

"You have a hat?" asked William.

The witch rushed to fetch it. It was black and pointed.

"That's a real goodun," approved William. "I'll show you how to fill it with money."

He dragged her down to the town. Showed her where to sit – outside the Town Hall, and what to sing. "It's a long way to Tipperary," he grunted, untunefully. "Pretend you're very old," he added.

"I *am* very old," snapped the witch.

"Pretend you're blind as well," said William.

"Gotcha," grinned the witch, screwing up her eyes and croaking out the song. She had pulled her grey hair over her face in order that she might not be recognized.

"Aaah," said people. "Oh dear," said some more, dropping odd coins into the witch's hat, and into William's. "Poor old things."

"This is *brilliant!*" exclaimed the witch.

". . . to Tipperary . . . keep on singing," hissed William.

He thought the witch's voice was even more appalling than his own, but she looked so dreadfully shabby, and so enormously old – it seemed to be bringing in the money.

"That'll do for now," interrupted William, hoarsely. "Time for a spot of lunch."

Abruptly forgetting that they were both deaf, lame and blind, he scurried off towards Macdonalds.

"Two cheeseburgers and chips," ordered William.

"With banana custard," added the witch, glinting through her matted hair.

"Er . . . "the girl said. "Are you sure you can pay?"

William produced a fifty pound note, blew some tobacco crumbs off it and slammed it down on the counter.

"Coming up," spluttered the Macdonald girl, rushing off.

"D'you mind if I smoke?" asked William when they were seated.

"D'you mind if I wash me socks in the teapot?" said the witch.

"By! You're a rum one!" grinned the tramp, appreciatively.

After their meal, William and the witch returned to the Town Hall and sang more terrible songs, like – "My Old Man's a Dustman", "She'll Be Coming

Round The Mountain", and "God Save Our Gracious Queen".

"We're *rich*!" chortled the witch, as they waddled home in the oncoming twilight. "You must stay the night."

The tramp looked around the witch's home: at the pretty patterns the cobwebs made around the ceiling sagging with the remains of dead flies and plump spiders; rotting cabbage leaves, heaving with caterpillars; and the dust which blew about in drifts in the draught. A bat sped out from behind the cooker, and George, who appeared to be asleep, whammed it with his paw.

"Cosy," said the tramp, "but I'm used to sleeping out of doors. Your nasturtium patch was most comfortable last night."

"Please yourself," sulked the witch. "I would have thought you'd've been grateful to sleep in a lovely home."

"Indeed I would! . . *normally*," muttered William the tramp, "but it's such a fine night . . . "

He shuffled off into the garden where it was beginning to rain, and lightning and thunder. But soon, he was snoring merrily with the splish splash of the rain on the nasturtium leaves above him, which were like many little green umbrellas.

The rain got worse, so that it was coming down like bullets out of a machine gun. The witch, worried about her guest's comfort, poked her head out of her bedroom window, wiggled her wand at the small nasturtium leaves and turned them into giant green umbrellas.

"By jove!" grunted William. "This garden is magic! *Absolutely bloomin' magic!*"

Next morning, he was rudely awakened by a great many clanging bells. He shot indoors, alarmed. "I think a new war has just started!" he puffed.

"It's Sunday," said the witch.

At that moment, Simon arrived. He was dressed, stiffly, in his Sunday best. With him was Angelica, who was looking like an angel in a sugar white frock. Angelica lived next door to Simon and it was not always possible to escape her. Especially on a Sunday when there was no Scouts, or shopping trips with his mother, or anything else.

"Goodness!" exclaimed Angelica when she espied the tramp. "Are you a wizard?"

William growled and Angelica felt a bit frightened. But her mother had told her always always to be kind to poor old people, and never never to be afraid, and this stopped Angelica from running away at once and she chirped, "We should *love* you to come to church with us. Wouldn't we, Simon?"

"Well . . . " Simon began, glancing at his friend the witch.

"And you too, . . . Mrs . . . Er" continued Angelica, shooting her sweetest smile at the witch. "We sing lots of super hymns."

"Hims? No hers?" asked the witch.

"She means sort of songs," explained Simon.

"Songs, you say?" asked the tramp. "Well what

are we waiting for?" He winked at the witch. "Grab your hat, Mrs!"

William and the witch did their best to sing their own songs, because they thought they were jollier than the ones everyone else was singing. And when they saw two men collecting money on a plate, they joined in with their hats.

"Disgusting!" gasped Lady Fox-Custard, glancing at the vicar as if he was a referee and should be giving the tramp and the witch a yellow card for foul behaviour.

She would just have to deal with it herself. At the end of the service, she wobbled after the disgusting pair, the fruit on her hat bouncing indignantly.

"Here, you!" She planted a fat hand on the tramp's shoulder and he spun round to look at her.

Lady Fox-Custard turned as white as a piece of paper and the fruit on the top of her hat all fell off.

"It's me long lost brother!" she gasped. "Sir William Fox-Custard; what on earth are you doing dressed like that?"

"SIR!" warbled Angelica, curtseying at once.

"A sir?" echoed Simon and Jimmy.

Lady Fox-Custard, who had not seen her brother since she had visited him in his magnificent mansion, spluttered like a whale out of water, "What are you doing with this *awful* woman?"

William was cross to hear his new friend so insulted so he said, "She's my girlfriend. We're getting married next week."

"Marrying that witch!" exclaimed Lady Fox-Custard, even more flabbergasted.

"Certainly he is," scoffed the witch, who couldn't believe her own ears. Or her mouth.

"And I'm going to be the bridesmaid," chirped Angelica, who now thought William was very sweet.

Simon and Jimmy were too astonished to say anything.

When they all arrived back at the witch's house, the witch was quite cross with William.

"Why did you pretend to be an old tramp?" she accused.

"I was just having an *experience*," said William.

No one understood that, so they didn't try.

What was more important, Simon said, was that they would *have* to get married now, or Lady Fox-Custard would scoff them silly.

"I don't mind," said Sir William, nobly.

"It'll be dead funny being called Lady William," tittered the witch. "My witch relations will be dreadfully jealous."

But Simon didn't like the idea.

"Poor old thing," said his mother that evening. "I must make her a dress. She must look nice on her wedding day."

Next day, the witch stood in the middle of Simon's living room whilst his mother walked round and round her with a length of white satin she'd bought cheaply, and with a mouthful of pins.

"Ow, ow!" the witch kept shrieking. "I'm not a bloomin' pin cushion."

"Sorry," puffed Simon's mother. "But you must stop walking about."

There was no money left over for a veil, but a piece of net curtain, pinned down with roses (which the witch intended to swop for nasturtiums) looked just as well.

"Golly!" she gasped, when she saw herself in the mirror. "Won't I make a fantastic bride!"

"Are you really sure you want to get married?" asked Simon.

"Doesn't *every* girl?" said the witch, batting her eyelashes preposterously.

The whole town was talking about the wedding

of the witch and Sir William. Especially Lady Fox-Custard.

"Of course, I shan't go." she snooted.

She told the mayor that *he* shouldn't go either. But the mayor said that, unfortunately, it was his *duty* to go. Secretly, he was greatly looking forward to it. Like everyone else, he was dying to see what the witch looked like in her bridal gown.

He rang the BBC and said they'd better bring their TV cameras if they wanted to see a sight for sore eyes.

He rang the Queen, but she said, "We are sorry, but we are washing our hair tomorrow."

Simon still did not want his friend to get married. Witches just *didn't*, he thought.

But the day arrived and everybody squashed into the church.

"Hey up!" boomed the witch. "Whose wedding is this?"

And her veil skidded to one side.

"Golly! She's early!" dithered Miss Crotchet, scampering to the organ and starting to play 'Here Comes the Bride'.

Sir William, who didn't want to look too fuddy duddy when he was marrying such an exciting lady, was wearing an open neck shirt with a gold medallion on his chest.

The TV cameras arrived.

Outside, and peering through the window, stood Lady Fox-Custard, wobbling dangerously on top of an orange box. She was grinding her teeth with rage and envy.

"Just think how *I* would look in that dress. *She* looks like an overgrown cauliflower," she scoffed.

The witch had just opened her mouth to say "I do," when one of her witch friends, called Hatty the Howl, burst through the door and yelled, "STOP! Important news!"

"Can't it wait?" the witch yelled back.

The excited camera men zoomed in closer with the boom. Lady Fox-Custard collapsed off her orange box and landed in a bed of nettles.

"S'too important," howled Hatty. "Come on!"

The witch said a hasty "Sorry" to Sir William and wobbled down the aisle and out of the door.

"Anyway," she puffed to herself, "who ever heard of a witch getting married? Witches just don't *do* that sort of thing."

Granny Grim's Cat

In a gloomy house, in a gloomy wood, sat one hundred witches. Their names too numerous to mention – except for Hatty the Howl, Sarah Screech, Winnie from Wapping, Minnie the Moan, and the witch herself. They were all swaying and swooning, screeching and squawking, moaning and groaning, whooping and howling and squashing one another.

In all the dark corners were rolling and blinking green eyes, belonging to the witches' cats. They were sharing out mice, playing patty-paws with the cobwebs and collecting spiders for the refreshments. George was sitting apart from the other cats, considering them common, counting the spiders and waiting for his opportunity to steal them.

"As you will all know," hooted Hatty, "except, that is, for *her* (she pointed to the witch) who I have just rescued from getting married, Great great great great great Granny Grim has died."

"It's so sad," wailed Winnie from Wapping. "She was only nine hundred years old. That's far too young to die."

"Oh do blow your nose!" scolded Hatty the Howl. "Granny Grim has left a will which I have to read."

"What's a will?" sniffed Winnie, wiping her nose on Hatty's sleeve.

"It's the opposite to a won't," cackled Sarah Screech.

Hatty scowled at her. "A will," she went on, "is a sort of letter with a list of things to be given away to friends and relations. After that person has died of course."

"Ooooooooooh!" cried all the witches at once. "Yippee whooee! Prezzies. It's just like Christmas!"

They crowded closer, pushing and scratching and stamping on one another. The noise was deafening. People in the town, far off, could hear it.

"I think there's a terrible storm coming," remarked Simon's mother. "I can hear the thunder rolling."

Simon and Jimmy ran into the garden to fetch in her washing. They too could hear the rumbling. Simon frowned. It didn't exactly sound like thunder to him.

"It's scarey," quivered Jimmy with a terrified grin.

Granny Grim had left a great many things in her will. There were millions of black stockings, some with hardly a hole in them. There were sticks and stones; bottles of poison; stuffed cats; pictures of cats; a dead ghost; a haunted chicken house; various claws and tails; an elephant's trunk, still with water in it; and many other useful things. To Hatty the Howl, she had left her broomstick (there were groans of envy at this). To Minnie the Moan, some bottled tears. To Sarah Screech, a screech owl. And to Winnie from Wapping, a whole sack full of frogs' legs – invaluable for using with magic spells.

"What about ME!?" cried the witch.

"Ah, yes," said Hatty. "There's a letter."

"I bet it's a 'Z'!" tittered Sarah.

Someone threw a cat at her.

"The letter," scowled Hatty, "says –

My dear great great great great great Grandchild,
Too yoo, I am leevin my veree fayvrut cat.
If yoo can luk after him wel for won munth –
I am leevin yoo a milliun.
Granny Grim.
xxxxx

The noise and whoops and growls, grunts and yawls and sobs that rose up from the hundred witches was so dreadful, that Lady Fox-Custard's prize begonias dropped dead on the spot and the mayor put on the tin hat he used to wear during the war.

The witch ran all the way home to Simon's house.

"I'm going to be a millionaire witch!" she shrieked. She hugged Simon's mother in her excitement. "All I've got to do is to look after one little pussy cat for a month, and Granny Grim is leavin' me a *million*! Oh, won't I be posh!"

"We're all terribly pleased for you," said Simon's mother. And she laid out some jam tarts. "What will you do with all that money?"

"I'll buy you a new washing machine, Mrs Woman," laughed the witch gaily, "and I'll buy Jimmy fifty pairs of roller skates, and I'll buy Simon a whole toy shop of his own."

"And what will you buy yourself?" asked Simon's mother.

A crafty look came into the witch's green eyes. "I'm gonna buy Horty Hall."

"But that belongs to Lady Fox-Custard!" exclaimed Simon.

"I know!" wheezed the witch, and she beezled off home to see if Granny Grim's cat had been delivered.

George was sitting on the doorstep to greet her. His fur was sticking up like barbed wire. He had a look on his face the witch had never seen before. It was a stricken look.

"What's up with *you*?" the witch asked.

George rolled his eyes in the direction of the living room. Sitting bolt upright on the hearthrug was an enormous animal.

It was bright yellow. Black stripes zoomed all over its back and belly. The talons on the ends of its paws were grinding up the rug into ribbons, and its whiskers were battle bent. When it smiled, its dagger-like fangs were black with age.

"You're a flippin', bloomin' TIGER!" gasped the witch.

The tiger, whose name was Christopher (long for Kitty), leapt at the witch and licked her all over. It seemed delighted to see her and to find himself in such a nice home.

The witch closed her eyes. Tight.

"I must be kind to it. I must be kind to this awful brute," she muttered.

The first thing to do was to feed the wretched animal.

Afraid to leave Christopher on his own, she made a leash from the washing line and set off towards the supermarket. The tiger padded along behind her, smelling everything and everybody. By the time they reached the shop, the streets were almost empty.

"Funny," muttered the witch. "It's not Sunday, is it?"

When she first went into the supermarket, it was quite full, but by the time she had filled her trolley with cat food, it was empty. There was not even a single girl at the check-out.

"*Very* odd," chunnered the witch. "Oh well, I'll pay next time. Maybe." And she trundled out with her shopping.

It was a long time since the witch had actually bought tinned cat meat and she was bothered about the whereabouts of her tin opener.

Christopher wasn't bothered. He scrunched up the food, tins and all and fell loudly asleep.

"Golly!" said the witch. "That's some cat! How am I going to look after that brute for a whole month? I think I'd rather have had some black stockings, or a dead ghost."

George would rather have had peace and quiet. He was a cat who had suffered much in his lifetime. He packed a few of his belongings – the remains of some table legs he had been saving for a rainy day, and skulked off to the gloomy house in the gloomy wood. He hadn't taken his holiday and now seemed a suitable time.

A few days later, the witch exclaimed, "Where's George?"

Christopher the tiger shrugged his yellow shoulders. Did the witch mean that miserable lump of dirty black fur? He waved a paw in several directions at once.

"Typical of George, that is," the witch snorted, " – to push off in several directions at once!"

She put the tiger on the leash again and took him to Simon's house.

Simon's mother opened the door and banged it shut again.

The witch pushed her nose through the window and said, "It's only me."

"But what about that tiger?" cried Simon's mother.

"Oh, you mean Christopher," said the witch. "Well he won't bite. At least as far as I know he doesn't."

The tiger leapt at the doorknob and swallowed it, which made it easier for the door to open.

He then raced in and sat himself down in front of the television where he remained glued, and fascinated.

The news came on, and there was a picture of the witch nearly getting married, and the tiger went round to the back of the set to find out how the witch managed to be inside this strange little box, and standing in the doorway, both at the same time.

At that moment, Simon and Angelica, who had been upstairs playing Scrabble, came running into the kitchen.

"Oooh!" exclaimed Angelica when she saw the tiger, "we've got a hearthrug like him! My daddy brought it back from India." She patted her curls. "My daddy's a Major General in the army and he simply *loves* shooting tigers and making them into rugs."

Christopher leapt up and ate Angelica's hair ribbon.

"Oh my goodness!" cried Angelica, going home to her mummy at once.

"I thought Granny Grim was leaving me a *cat*," moaned the witch when Angelica had disappeared.

"Well, I suppose he *is* a cat," said Simon. "Lions and panthers and jaguars and tigers are all cats. They're just bigger."

"I like small cats," sulked the witch. "And how do you suppose I'm going to look after that monstrosity for a whole month?"

Whilst she was busy moaning, Christopher, who

had grown bored of Simon's house, and also, hadn't liked Angelica's remarks about the tiger rugs, loped off through the open kitchen door.

He found the English countryside quite charming. The people were charming – they all made way for him. All he had to do, was to snarl in a friendly way, show his aged black teeth, and he had the whole town to himself. First he went back to the supermarket and finished off the shelves of cat food. He went to the cinema to see the 'Pink Panther' and was surprised that no one asked him to pay. He went to see the mayor, who said he was busy. The vicar was making up some magnificent sermons and bolting his back door. Christopher arrived at a beautiful garden which had a lovely goldfish pond. He was hungry and thirsty by now, so he drank the pond and ate the fish. Full to bursting, he fell asleep in a tall oak tree; the property, as it happened, of Lady Fox-Custard.

"Where's Granny Grim's tiger?" asked Simon, suddenly.

"Oh! Xmas crackers!" exclaimed the witch. "That over-sized moggy's worth a fortune! Here kitty, kitty," she cried, searching all round Simon's house and garden and down the road and back again.

"He's gone!" she shrieked. "I'm *ruined*."

"Oh dear," said Simon's mother, feebly.

When it was dark, the witch gave up and went home. The tiger was a hungry animal. It was bound to turn up soon. But a week went by and there was no sign of him.

Meanwhile, Lady Fox-Custard was having problems of her own. She had been down to feed her goldfish and found the whole pond missing.

"Cripes!" she exclaimed, forgetting for a moment that she was a lady. "Where's me fish gorn?"

There was a flump behind her as Christopher fell out of the tree and started to smell this fat lady in the flowered dress. He nibbled one of the flowers to see if it was nice and spat it out. It was the first nylon flower he had tasted and he thought it was nasty.

Lady Fox-Custard shot towards the house to phone the police and Christopher shot after her.

"Come quickly!" she screamed. "I've got a tiger in my house!"

"Oh yes," said Constable Scuff, who didn't believe her, "and what's it doing there?"

"It's sitting in my armchair. It's eating my chocolates. It'll be eating *me* if you don't hurry up."

"Just coming, your Ladyship," mumbled Constable Scuff, finishing his cucumber sandwich and going to the washroom to comb his moustache.

"Whatever next. Flippin' tigers!" he remarked, twitching out a stray hair. He straightened his helmet, had another look in the mirror at his handsome face, and drove off in a leisurely manner to Horty Hall.

During this time, Christopher, who had enjoyed Lady Fox-Custard's chocolates enormously, especially the coffee creams, had taken a fancy to the fat lady. He put a heavy yellow paw round her shoulder and beamed at her, toothily. He licked her curls, which oddly fell straight. He adored the smell of her perfume, which was called L'eau de Crumpet. Lady Fox-Custard stood perfectly still. It was as if she was frozen to the spot. By the time Constable Scuff arrived, Lady Fox-Custard's hair had gone completely straight, the nylon flowers on her dress had dropped dead, and she was as white as a ghost – on account of Christopher having eaten all her make-up.

"Blimey!" exclaimed Constable Scuff, reaching swiftly for his radio and talking into it sideways,

"Emergency. Horty Hall. Van with dogs required. Roger."

There followed a great noise of sirens, car horns, shouting policemen, and yapping Alsatians. The tiger

thought it was great. He instantly made friends with the dogs and was happy to go with them. But to his dismay, he was put in a cage and locked up. He wondered miserably where he was.

"You're in the zoo," said a moth-eaten lion next to him. "Supper isn't until seven."

Christopher was fed up, and so was the witch.

"All that money I was gonna get," she moaned to Simon. "Just vanished."

"I wouldn't give up yet," Simon said. "Tigers don't get lost that easily. We are bound to hear about him soon."

And indeed they did.

There were big pictures of Lady Fox-Custard in all the newspapers, and she was on television that very same evening. By this time, she had re-curled her hair and was wearing a huge poppy dress.

"My goodness!" she was saying. "I caught him by the tail and hung onto him until the police came. He tried to claw me with his terrible paws, but I biffed him on the nose and wrestled the terrible creature to the ground."

An hour later, she was talking to Mr Wogan. She had changed into some trousers and was wearing her diamond tiara.

"Yes, Terry," she went on, patting his knee, "he would have eaten me alive, but I twisted his ears, pulled his tail, and *sat* on him."

"Did you really!" exclaimed Terry Wogan.

"Yes, really," said Lady Fox-Custard. "And of course, because I am so terribly fond of animals,

I did not kill the monster, but had him taken to the zoo."

"The *zoo!*" cried the witch, flying there at once.

"I've come to fetch my animal," she puffed.

"Which animal?" asked the zoo keeper.

"Yes," said the witch.

"Yes, what?" asked the zoo keeper.

"What you just said," snapped the witch. "A witch animal. A tiger called Christopher."

"We've got lots of tigers here," sighed the zoo keeper.

"This one's yellow and it's got black stripes zooming all over its back and under its belly."

"A normal tiger shape," scoffed the zoo keeper.

"And it eats tins, and nylon flowers and has been talked about by Terry Wogan," explained the witch.

"Oh, *that* one!" cried the zoo keeper. "You're welcome to take him away at once. He's been a dreadful nuisance."

The witch was about to grab Christopher and take him home, when the tiger, who was not ready to give up his freedom and be taken back to the witch's squashy old kitchen, shot off towards the dark and gloomy wood, leaving the witch gasping and muttering terrible oaths.

The Dark and Gloomy Wood

The witch stomped home, chunnering about lost millions and mad, ungrateful tigers. And Christopher padded on, deeper and deeper into the dark and gloomy wood.

He was a tiger who was used to the bright jungle, where huge flowers grew and cheerful birds of every colour, chirped and squawked. Here, there was nothing but gloom and doom. The silence was awesome. Moving his way stealthily through the trees he came across many strange objects. There were half eaten torn black stockings, chicken bones and feathers, the remains of a ghost, worn and damp around the edges, and a haunted chicken house which was wailing and moaning as if it had a pain under its floorboards.

The tiger's stripes, which ran all over its back and under its belly, shuddered.

Further on in the gloomy wood, he came upon

a small, dark house. He imagined he saw a mangy looking cat with one red eye and one green, leaping out of an open window and disappearing into the darkness. As it happened, this was George, the witch's long suffering cat. At the sight of the large yellow monster, who had moved into his home and onto his favourite hearthrug, George had decided to escape. He had no wish to stay and be friendly with it.

"Oh gosh!" thought Christopher, "this is the nastiest, darkest, gloomiest, most unfriendly place I have ever seen."

He was in the middle of thinking this, when a most delicious smell snorted up his nostrils. It was the smell of crackling bacon and eggs. It was coming from the inside of the gloomy house.

"Yo ho hummy,
Scrummy yummy tummy,"

sang an old man with a frying pan. It was the tramp. The very same tramp who had nearly married the witch.

Christopher the tiger, edged his hungry nose a little further over the windowsill.

"Hullo, you big yellow pussy cat," greeted the tramp in a most friendly and unfrightened way.

Christopher slid his big front paws on to the window sill, and then his back paws, until all of him was inside the dark and gloomy house.

To his pleasant surprise, the old tramp did not seem to mind. He just carried on turning the eggs

and crisping the bacon. Now he was frying two
slices of fried bread and throwing tea bags into an
old brown pot.

"Sit down, big fella," he was saying. "There's
plenty here for the two of us. As a matter of fact, I
was feeling a bit lonely until you came along. Sugar
in your tea?"

"Grrrrrres," growled Christopher, happily, drinking the tea at once and then crunching up the cup
as well.

"Now if you're going to stay with *me*, stripey
puss," scolded the tramp, "you'll have to learn
better manners than THAT!"

No one before, had ever told the tiger that he should learn manners. He thought it would be quite nice to learn something new – whatever manners were. This strange old man he had been lucky enough to meet must be a Manners Teacher.

"Lesson one," continued the tramp, "you don't eat the cups. Or the plates. And you don't lick the table or blow your nose on the napkins."

Christopher looked greatly surprised at all this, but he grinned and nodded his head vigorously. Joyfully, he leapt across the table and licked the tramp's face.

"And you don't lick people, either," scolded the tramp again, yet secretly pleased that the big tiger seemed to like him so much.

After their supper, they sat by a small fire the tramp had managed to light and looked around their new home, contentedly. The firelight showed them all sorts of strange objects. Objects which had been left behind by the hundred witches. It was a good job that neither the tramp nor the tiger was afraid. There were extra large spiders everywhere. They were as big as crabs. Some of them had orange eyes. Some green, and others red. And they blinked on and off like traffic lights and stared in a very unfriendly way. The witches had left an old dart board, and on it hung dead mice. Pinned by their tails. A pair of yellow teeth chattered across the floor, but there was nobody attached to them. Christopher sniffed the yellow teeth and got bitten on the nose. Crossly, he smashed them with his paw and they rolled away in pieces, screeching,

"Woe to you, bad witch's cat.
Granny Grim shall hear of this . . . hear of
this . . . . . . hear of this."

"Granny *Grim!*" hissed the spiders.
"Tomorrow," swore the tramp, "I'm going to buy
a Hoover and suck up all these pesky creatures.
They have no *manners.*"

The tiger was pleased to hear this. He felt safe
and cosy with the Manners Teacher. Then his
whiskers began to tremble with weariness and the
next minute he was snoring deeply. The tramp
started to snore too, and the dark and dismal house
in the middle of the dark and gloomy wood shook
with strange sounds, added to by the miaows
of cats under the floorboards and hidden in the
rafters. They were witches' cats who had escaped
from their owners and were trying to have a bit of
a holiday before they were recaptured.

Next morning, the tramp went into town to buy
a Hoover.

The shop man looked at the tramp's ragged
clothes, and scoffed, "Cash, or cheque, Sir?"

"I'll pay by cheque," said the tramp. And he
signed his name, WILLIAM FOX-CUSTARD.

The man in the shop went purple, and then
white, and gasped, "Of *course*, Sir William. At *once*,
Sir William. Will you be able to carry it, or shall I
have it delivered?"

"I'll take it now," the tramp said. And he whistled

for Christopher who was waiting outside.

He tied the Hoover to the tiger's back, raised his tattered cap to the shop man, who had slid under the counter in a dead faint, and walked home.

The spiders were furious when they saw the Hoover being switched on, and scrambled and wriggled to escape. But Christopher roared and

growled so fiercely, they all raced towards the Hoover and were sucked up. A furry bat, curious to see what was going on, flumped down from the ceiling and was slurped up too. Last of all, the chattery yellow teeth rattled up the tube.

"And let's hope that's the end of *them!*" said the tramp. And he hammered a sign on the front door which said,

This is the residence of
Sir William Fox-Custard. T.R.A.M.P

All this time, the witch was storming around the town feeling distraught.

"*I'm distraught!*" she wailed to Simon. "I nearly had a *million* in my hands and now it's escaped!"

"He can't have gone far," comforted Simon.

"Oh no!" scoffed the witch. "Only somewhere like Africa. I bet he's sitting in the jungle right now, eatin' bananas and enjoyin' himself."

"But he couldn't have got there," said Simon, trying to calm down his friend.

"*Couldn't he!*" screeched the witch. "He's a *witch's* cat. He was Granny *Grim's* cat. Who knows what he couldn't do? He's not just an ordinary cat. He might have had his own transport for all *we* know."

"What sort of transport?" stuttered Simon. He had never seen the witch so mad.

"Well, not a jet plane, or a motor bike, or a corporation bus . . . a *broomstick* of course, you silly boy. He could zoom across any ocean if he had a broomstick. He was Granny *Grim's* cat. He might have had a special jet-propelled, supersonic, de-luxe, one thousand horse-power broomstick. Granny Grim could've given it to him for his birthday. He could've zoomed supersonically to any distant land by now and I'll be a poor old woman again."

Simon was interested. He could just imagine the big yellow tiger, supersonicking round the world. Diving behind the moon. Nearly, but not quite, crashing into the stars.

"Well?" snapped the witch.

Simon jumped down out of his dream and said, "Maybe he's just been stolen."

"*Stolen!*" exploded the witch. "Who would want to steal a stupid yellow lump like him?"

"Another witch perhaps," Simon suggested.

"Another witch? . . . another witch, you say?" cried the witch. "You could be right."

She grabbed her telephone book and looked up 'W' for witches. She rang all the witches she knew and all the ones she didn't. But no one had stolen her tiger.

"Who would *want* it, dear heart?" howled Hatty. "But darling, if you don't find him before Friday, you are going to lose the million. Friday is the last day of the month."

"I know!" wailed the witch.

Feverishly, she rang her sister, Tombola, in Africa.

Tombola was in the middle of washing her hair

and she had coconut shampoo in her ears.

"Have you got me tiger?" yelled the witch.

"Yes, I did have," puffed Tombola. "But the ointment worked wonderfully. I'm much better now thank you."

"Phaw!" snorted the witch, turning purple, and green, and orange. "I'm talking about a *tiger*. Have you got him?"

"I've got dozens of tigers," Tombola said. "The garden's full of them. They keep eatin' the roof."

"This one's got black stripes zooming all over its back and under its belly."

Tombola plodded out into her garden and back again.

"They all have," she shouted.

"This one's called Christopher."

"Tombola stumped back into the garden.

"Christopher!" she yelled.

"Christopher?" the tigers thought. "What a silly name for a tiger."

And they covered their mouths with their paws and sniggered.

"No," said Tombola. "He ain't here."

The witch tore at her shaggy hair and moaned. "It's Thursday tomorrow," she said to Simon. "Where else can I look?"

"We'll get up really early in the morning and search the whole town again," said Simon hurriedly, and he went home.

The witch was just starting to snore, when an extra large spider crawled under the bedroom door.

It had enormous red eyes which lit up the whole room. Its eight legs were bent and twisted and its body was covered in fluff – just as if it had crawled out of the inside of a Hoover. The witch gawped at it, hungrily. But the spider was muttering, peevishly. It seemed to be saying, "Granny Grim . . . Granny Grim."

"Cripes!" exclaimed the witch. "A *witch's* spider! That's somewhere I haven't looked yet."

Next morning, she greeted Simon, excitedly.

"We're going to the dark and gloomy wood," she cried.

"Do we *have* to?" asked Simon.

"Yes, we do have to," said the witch. "I've got a funny feeling under my vest about it."

"So have I!" shivered Simon.

The tramp and the tiger had finished cleaning the house and were gardening hard. The tramp was clipping the bushes into posh shapes. He was doing peacocks and castles and flamingoes and Alsatians.

"You sweep up the clippings, Christopher lad," he told the tiger.

"Grrrrall Grrrright," grinned the tiger. And he munched up all the fallen leaves and twigs.

His mouth was crammed full when Simon and the witch appeared.

"*There* you are!" boomed the witch. "You sneaky, disobedient, ungrateful, brainless, stupid lump of yellow trouble!"

"Grrrroo? grrrree??" mumbled the tiger.

"Yes, *you*," screamed the witch. "I've been looking for you everywhere. I've been distraught. It's nearly *Friday*."

The tiger looked puzzled.

"Hold on," interrupted the tramp. "This lovely animal is my friend. I don't like you calling him horrid names."

"You can keep him then – after tomorrow, and I'm jolly glad I didn't marry a tiger thief," snorted the witch.

But when Simon had explained the whole story; about Granny Grim's will, and how the witch was going to get a million if she managed to look after the tiger for a month, everyone understood and went indoors for morning coffee and muffins.

"And you promise I can keep him after tomorrow?" asked the tramp.

"Oh defnully!" exclaimed the witch.

On Friday, Hatty The Howl came to inspect the witch's house and to see that she was still looking after the tiger.

The tiger was purr-grurring happily on the mat and his whiskers were crisp and clean.

"Well done!" hooted Hatty. "Your million is waiting for you in the middle of the football pitch. I'll meet you there." And she shot off.

"What a stupid place to leave a million!" gasped the witch. "Someone might pinch it." And she raced after Hatty.

But a terrible sight met her eyes. The whole of the pitch was yellow with tigers, all with black stripes zooming across their backs and under their bellies. Hatty was prodding them and keeping them in order and stopping them from escaping.

"What's *this*?" shrieked the witch, frantically. "Granny Grim promised me a million."

"There *are* a million," scolded Hatty. "I've just counted them."

"I thought she meant a million pounds!" wailed the witch, "not a million tigers."

"Don't you like them?" asked Hatty, surprised, and thinking how ungrateful the witch was.

"They're all right, I suppose," sulked the witch, "if you like tigers. But I just haven't got room for

them all".

"Oh," said Hatty The Howl, unfeelingly. And she sped off on her broomstick.

The witch went to find Simon and Jimmy.

"What am I going to do with them all?" she asked.

"Hec!" said Jimmy when he saw them. "Bloomin' hec!"

"You could sell them," suggested Simon. "Put an advert in the newspaper." And he helped the witch to write out an advertisement.

For a long time, no one answered, and no one felt like playing football either. Most people stayed indoors and watched television.

Then, one hot sunny day, a Rolls Royce rolled up to the witch's door and a man wearing a tablecloth on his head, climbed down and said, "I am Sheik Phatso and I have come to buy your tigers."

"What, ALL of them!?" gasped the witch.

"If you can spare them," said the sheik. "I have umpteen palaces and a million wives, and I need some tigers to guard them."

"Well . . . " said the witch, pretending to think about it. "They're a pound each you know. They're very good quality tigers. I've had a lot of important people asking about them."

"A pound each is OK." said the sheik.

And he paid the witch at once.

The witch felt quite dizzy. When she felt better, she rang Simon and yelled, "I'm a MILLIONAIRE WITCH! I really am!"

While she was speaking, George, who had had enough of the dark and gloomy wood, came shiftily through the open door. At the same time, something plopped through the witch's letter box. It was her new old age pension book.

"And about time too!" snorted the witch. And she spread it with marmalade and gave it to George for his tea.

That done, she waddled off to buy Horty Hall.

Even Lady Fox-Custard wouldn't be able to argue with a millionaire witch.